Monster Mountain

Thunderbelle's Beauty Parlour

For Reuben Carolan
K.W.
For Holly and Joel,
with love
G. P-R.

First published in 2007 by Orchard Books
First paperback publication in 2008

ORCHARD BOOKS
338 Euston Road, London NW1 3BH
Orchard Books Australia
Level 17/207 Kent St, Sydney, NSW 2000

ISBN 978 1 84362 623 7 (hardback)
ISBN 978 1 84362 631 2 (paperback)

1 3 5 7 9 10 8 6 4 2 (hardback)
1 3 5 7 9 10 8 6 4 2 (paperback)

Printed in China

Orchard Books is a division of Hachette Children's Books,
an Hachette Livre UK company.

www.orchardbooks.co.uk

Monster Mountain

Thunderbelle's Beauty Parlour

Karen Wallace

Illustrated by

Guy Parker-Rees

ORCHARD BOOKS

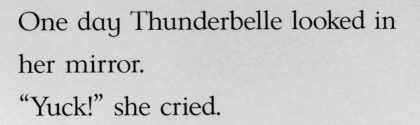

One day Thunderbelle looked in
her mirror.
"Yuck!" she cried.

5

"My nose is too bumpy!
My horns are too rough!
My legs look like tree trunks!
I don't want to see myself
ever again!"

She put a tablecloth over her head
And cut two holes so she could
see out.

The other monsters were very
worried.

"Why is Thunderbelle wearing
a tablecloth over her head?"
asked Roxorus.

"Maybe she's going to have
a special tea party," said Clodbuster.
"Don't be silly!" squawked
Pipsquawk. "Tablecloths are for
tables! You don't wear them on
your head!"

Mudmighty chewed his muddy lips.
"I think Thunderbelle is unhappy,"
he said.

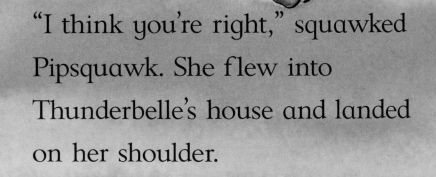

"I think you're right," squawked
Pipsquawk. She flew into
Thunderbelle's house and landed
on her shoulder.

At first Thunderbelle wouldn't talk.

She grunted.

She snorted.

Then she sighed a big sigh. A tear dribbled down from under the tablecloth. It landed with a PLOP on the floor.

"What's wrong?" whispered
Pipsquawk.

Thunderbelle sniffed.

Then she gulped.

Then she told Pipsquawk how she
didn't like herself any more.

"Is that why you are wearing
a tablecloth on your head?"
asked Pipsquawk.
Thunderbelle nodded.

Pipsquawk hung upside down from
a lamp. Pipsquawk had her best
ideas upside down.

Then she flew down the mountain
and rang the Brilliant Ideas gong.
Bong! Bong! Bong!

Clodbuster bounced up
on his pogo stick.

Roxorus zoomed in
on his skateboard.

Mudmighty slipped
all the way down.

Thunderbelle came as quickly as she could, even though she was wearing the tablecloth on her head.

All the monsters stared at
Thunderbelle. No one knew
what to say.
"What's the matter?" asked
Roxorus at last.

"Thunderbelle doesn't like herself any more," explained Pipsquawk. She hopped about on a branch. "Everyone feels like that sometimes."

"So what's your brilliant idea?"
asked Clodbuster.

"We'll open a beauty parlour!"
cried Pipsquawk. "We'll make
Thunderbelle the most beautiful
monster on Monster Mountain!"

Everyone clapped and cheered.
"Pipsquawk! You're a genius!"
they cried.

That day, the monsters were very
busy. They collected leafy branches
and pink flowers and made
a beauty parlour.

Clodbuster built Thunderbelle
a comfortable
chair to sit on.

Mudmighty mixed
up the best mud
face-mask ever.

And Roxorus
brought his special
exercise wheel.

When they were finished,
Thunderbelle took the
tablecloth off.
"Ready?" squawked Pipsquawk.
"Ready," said Thunderbelle.

First Roxorus showed
Thunderbelle how to pedal his
special wheel.
It was amazing! Thunderbelle was
sure her legs looked better already!

Then Thunderbelle climbed into her chair and Mudmighty put a mud mask on her face. "This will get rid of all those lumps and bumps," he said.

Pipsquawk rubbed special cream
into Thunderbelle's horns.
"Now they will be nice and
smooth," she said.

Thunderbelle leaned back and
closed her eyes.
It was lovely to be fussed over.

At last she stood up and stared in
the mirror.

"You look beautiful," said
Clodbuster.

"Fabulous," said Roxorus.

"Gorgeous," said Mudmighty.

"I LOOK exactly the same as always!" laughed Thunderbelle. "But I FEEL a million times better!"

Monster Mountain

All priced at £8.99. Monster Mountain books are available from
all good bookshops, or can be ordered direct from the publisher:
Orchard Books, PO BOX 29, Douglas IM99 1BQ. Credit card orders
please telephone 01624 836000 or fax 01624 837033 or visit our website:
www.orchardbooks.co.uk or e-mail: bookshop@enterprise.net for details.

To order please quote title, author and ISBN and your full name and address.
Cheques and postal orders should be made payable to 'Bookpost plc.'
Postage and packing is FREE within the UK
(overseas customers should add £2.00 per book).

Prices and availability are subject to change.